Makana is a G[ift]
is dedicated to our prec[ious]
carrying their peaceful vibration
throughout the waters of the earth;
and to all who love and protect them.

The name *Makana* means *gift*
in the beautiful Hawaiian language.

Life is a gift, and so are you.

Swim with peace!
Love,
Janet

SEVEN SEAS
PRESS

MAKANA
is a Gift

written by
Janet Lucy

illustrated by
Alexis Cantu

The sun glistened on the water like gold glitter,
where a little green sea turtle was basking on the surface
of the warm turquoise water of Turtle Cove.

The little green sea turtle
had arrived in the cove the night before
after his long swim through the open ocean.

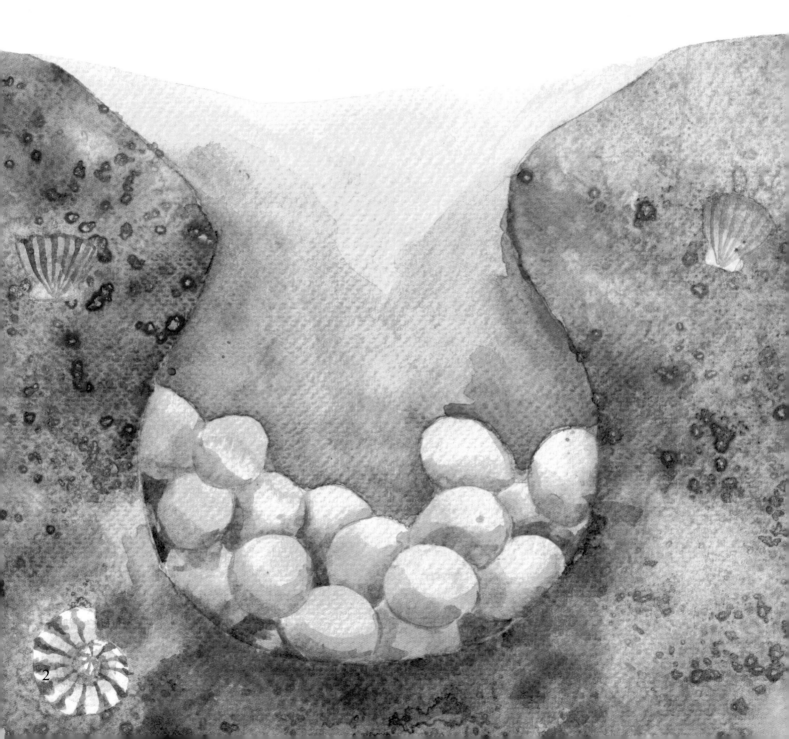

He was born from a round white egg
the size of a ping pong ball
in a nest with 100 other tiny turtles on the shore,
where his mother had laid them
deep in the sand to protect them.

The eggs had incubated safely in their nest
warmed by the sun for two months,
while their shells and flippers formed,
as well as the markings that make
each green sea turtle distinct.

As soon as the eggs cracked open,
the two-inch hatchlings climbed out of their sandy cradle,
then made their slow and steady crawl to the ocean.

When the hatchlings finally reached the water,
they began separate adventures,
each finding their way out to sea,
guided by the moon and starlight reflecting on the water.

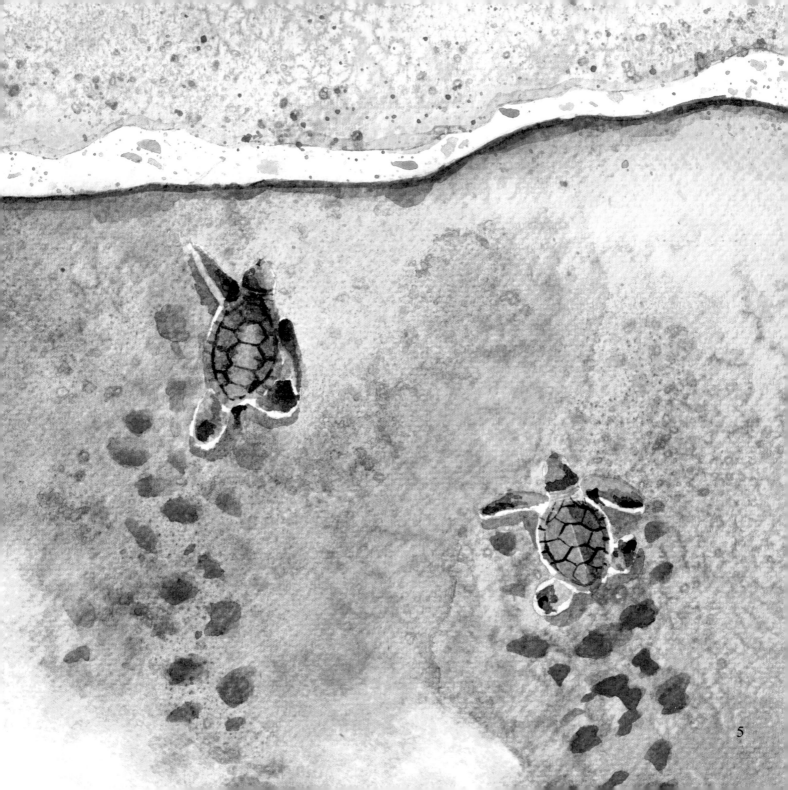

It had taken the little green sea turtle six years
swimming in the open ocean,
navigating by instinct,
eating and growing amongst floating seaweed,
until he finally reached the cove,
hundreds of miles away from where he was born.

The little green sea turtle was tired
when he arrived in Turtle Cove!

He was still small, his smooth brown
heart-shaped shell, 14-inches long,
streaked with a sunburst pattern
in brilliant yellow and gold.

He gently bobbed on the surface,
his head and flippers hanging down,
the sun casting rays of light below him.

The little green sea turtle opened his eyes.
He was not alone!
The cove was already home
to other green sea turtles much bigger than him.

The little green sea turtle felt a stirring below him.
An enormous turtle poked his head out of his shell,
where he slept wedged on a ledge
for protection in the deeper water.

"Welcome, early riser. I see you are a new arrival.
They call me Kato. What do we call you?"

"I don't have a name yet," the little green sea turtle told him.

"Then we'll have to wait and see who you are," Kato told him.

The little green sea turtle nodded.

"Rest and eat up," the elder turtle advised him.
"You've come a long way."

The little green sea turtle could see
there was plenty of red and green algae
covering the coral reef.
He'd found the perfect habitat.

He foraged on the reef for breakfast, then found a ledge,
tucked himself in and drifted dreamily off to sleep.

Later in the afternoon
the little green sea turtle woke up
and decided to go exploring.

Here in Turtle Cove he saw
a spiky starfish stuck tightly onto a rock.
Colorful schools of shimmering fish zipped by him.
A zebra-striped eel peeked out
from a narrow crevice.

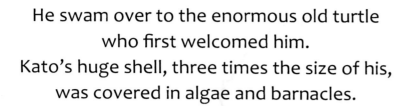

He swam over to the enormous old turtle
who first welcomed him.
Kato's huge shell, three times the size of his,
was covered in algae and barnacles.

The little green sea turtle watched
as bright yellow fish fed on
the algae and barnacles on Kato's shell.
He wished they'd swim to him,
but his shell was still smooth and glossy
without any food on it.

When he tried to join them, they darted away.

Oh, he thought, *if only I were a fish
and could swim in the school with them.*

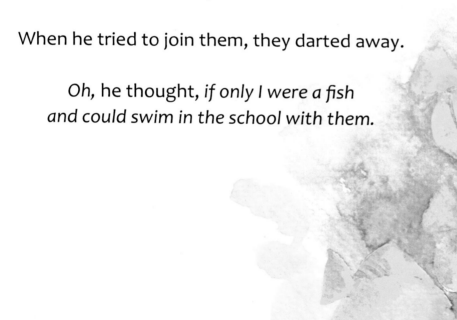

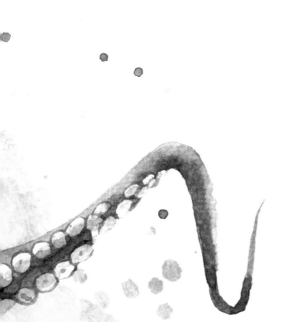

The little green sea turtle was fascinated
by a big brown beautiful octopus.
He approached her curiously.
He marveled at her eight arms.
Imagine, he thought, *what one could do
with arms like that!*

When he moved in closer, she changed colors!
"How do you do that?" he asked her.

She blushed, changing colors again.
If only he could change colors, too!

"It's camouflage," the octopus explained.
"It keeps me safe."

"You have your own unique color and
design to protect you," she assured him.

"I'm Helena," she added, extending a tentacle.

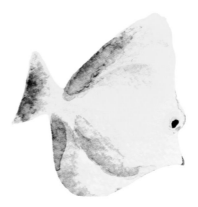

The little green sea turtle actually wasn't green
as his species' name implied.

He was a blend of different colors—
his shell was shades of brown, olive and gold
that would keep changing as he grew older.
His under shell was yellowish-white.
His head, a mosaic of brown and yellow markings.

The little green sea turtle loved to bask
near the surface of the water
where he could feel the sun on his shell.

Floating and bobbing, he was lifted by a wave.
Oh, how happy he felt!

Suddenly the ocean surged—
the little green sea turtle was tossed about,
spinning dizzily.
He crashed into the coral. *Oooof!*

If only I could cling to the rocks like the starfish,
or had tentacles, like Helena the octopus, he thought.

The little green sea turtle popped his head up and took a bite of air.

He saw seabirds circling overhead.
He heard the cries of the white gulls and grey terns.

He flapped his flippers back and forth beneath the surface of the water.

If only these were wings, and I could fly! Feel the freedom in the sky!

The little green sea turtle felt motion below him.
Kato was awake, preparing for his evening forage.

He dove down to find him.
The yellow tang and blue parrotfish feeding on
Kato's shell darted away again.

The little green sea turtle swam away too,
feeling lonely and confused.
Would he ever make friends and find his place
of belonging in Turtle Cove?

Why am I here, and so different? he mused.
That night, the little green sea turtle
tossed and turned in his sleep,
dreaming of his life in the open sea.

The next morning, the first light of dawn illuminated the surface of the water.
The little green sea turtle woke up hungry, as always.

To his delight, he spotted a clear and luminous jelly drifting by. Breakfast!

The little green sea turtle loved jellyfish.
He'd survived on them during his long years in the open sea,
and hadn't seen one since he arrived in the cove.

He eagerly swam over and took a big hungry bite!

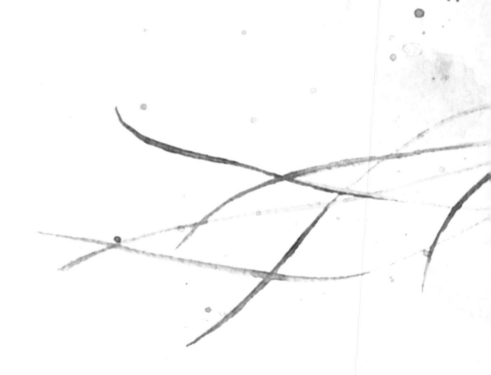

27

Wait! What was this? It didn't dissolve like the other jellies.
After he sucked it in, it stuck in his throat!
The little green sea turtle choked! He couldn't breathe!
What could he do? He needed help!

He dove down in search of Kato.

The big jellyfish was still floating over his head, obstructing his view.

He couldn't see as the jelly's billowy body covered his eyes.

Now he was down deep,
Kato surely asleep,
and he would need a breath of air soon.

He flapped his flippers, swimming in circles … now he was woozy, too!
Which way was up? Where was the surface?

Just then, something darted toward him, like strands of brown seaweed —
What was it?

Then he heard the familiar voice of Helena, the octopus.
"My goodness, dear one, that's quite a mouthful you've taken in."

Helena grasped the plastic bag with her tentacles, suctioned tightly,
then began to gently pull and slowly ease away from him.

The little green sea turtle choked a bit more as the bag moved through his throat,
then he coughed it out of his mouth.

When he opened his eyes, Helena was watching him closely,
changing colors as emotions pulsed through her body.

"You gave me quite a fright," she told him,
the plastic bag now securely in her grasp,
wrapped in one of her tentacles.

32

The little green sea turtle swam quickly to the surface
for a desperate breath of air and gulped it in.

He looked around—so happy to see
the birds circling overhead,
the vast blue sky, the bright morning sun.

A wave of gratitude washed through him.

He dove back down in search of Helena.

Instead he found Kato swimming toward him.

"Helena saved my life," he told him.

"She did, indeed," Kato affirmed.

"What would I have done without her,
without her long arms and tentacles?"
the little green sea turtle wondered.

Kato nodded, thoughtfully.

"Have you ever wished you were someone else?"
the little green sea turtle asked Kato.

"Yes, I do remember wishing to be a dolphin,
leaping out of the water and spinning playfully in the air," Kato admitted.

"We all search to discover who and why we are—
to know our purpose and our value in this world.
In time you will understand yours.

I'll tell you this much—

"We are survivors, the oldest species still alive
since the dinosaurs roamed the earth with our ancestors.
We have been here a very long time, and I trust you will be too.

Did you know, you might live to be 100 years old, as I have?

You are still quite young and restless,
but we sea turtles are the wisdom keepers.

You still have a long life ahead of you.
You will make many more journeys
traveling through the ocean, returning to your birthplace.

Your job is to be true to your nature, carrying our peaceful vibration.
There is no other species like us, and no other green sea turtle like you."

The little green sea turtle listened carefully.

"We're all different," Kato continued.

"We all have a unique purpose.
We're all needed here to help and care for each other."

"Life is a gift, isn't it?" the little green sea turtle replied.

"Yes, life is a gift," Kato nodded, "and so are you.

We'll call you Makana."

Makana basked in the sun
on the surface of the water,
drenched in the gold glitter,
warmed with the wisdom and certainty,
there was no one else he'd rather be, than himself.

DISCUSSION & ACTIVITIES GUIDE

Identity & Community

1. Makana means "gift" in Hawaiian. Makana received his name from Kato after discovering his life and unique nature are a gift. What are some of his gifts and unique features? What are some of yours? If you were given a name that describes you, what might it be? Does your name have a meaning?

2. At one point in the story Makana asks Kato, "Have you ever wished you were someone else?" Have you ever felt this way?

3. Makana wondered, *Would he ever make friends and find his place of belonging in Turtle Cove?* Have you ever been new in a school or group? If so, how did you feel?

4. The turtles and other creatures in Turtle Cove are like a family, though not related to each other biologically. Do you have a group of friends who feel like family to you?

5. Makana has a special friend, Helena, the octopus. She's a different species. Do you have friends who aren't like you? How are they different? How are you alike?

6. Helena the octopus became an invaluable friend to Makana, noticing when he was in trouble and quickly coming to his aid. How do you identify who can help you? Who are the people in your life who help you and care for you? Who in your community can you help and take care of?

7. Kato was the biggest, oldest turtle in the cove, 100 years old. He is a wise elder. Do you know someone like Kato? Kato tells Makana that sea turtles are the "wisdom keepers." What do you think a wisdom keeper is?

8. Sea turtles navigate by instinct—the guiding senses in the body. How do you use your senses? How do you use your instincts to guide you?

9. A sea turtle's shell has a pattern, viewed by Native American cultures as 13 moons, each said to hold its own story. Imagine you are like a sea turtle and you have 13 stories you carry with you. Would you like to tell one? Children might enjoy crafting their own book of 13 stories.

10. Art activity: Draw, paint or collage a sea turtle; or create an undersea scene from your favorite mediums. Consider mixed media for more texture and dimension.

Ecology & Protection ~ Food for Thought for All of Us

11. Plastic bags and plastic straws are particularly dangerous to sea turtles, as they can get stuck in their throats and noses. What could you use as alternatives?

12. If you live near a beach or a waterway, plan a plastic clean up day with your friends, family or classmates.

13. Cruise the aisles of your local grocery store. Notice how much plastic is used for packaging. What could be used as an alternative? Where could you buy produce and other foods and products in bulk?

14. Pack your lunch plastic-free. What alternative containers can you take your food and drinks in?

15. "Plastic Free July" is a global movement created to bring awareness to the quantity of "single use" plastics we use daily and other plastic products polluting our environment. Single-use plastics include plastic shopping bags, plastic cups, straws, plastic packaging, and anything intended to be used once and then discarded. *Would you like to take the challenge?*

RESOURCES

People and Organizations that Protect Sea Turtles & their Environment

SAVE THE SEA TURTLES INTERNATIONAL savetheseaturtlesinternational.org

SEE TURTLES seeturtles.org/sea-turtles-plastic

SEA TURTLE CONSERVANCY conserveturtles.org/sea-turtle-conservancy

OCEANIC SOCIETY oceanicsociety.org/resources/7-ways-to-reduce-ocean-plastic-pollution-today/

CHRISTINE FIGGENER, PHD. seaturtlebiologist.com/about

PLASTIC FREE MERMAID ~ I QUIT PLASTICS iquitplastics.com

PLASTIC FREE JULY plasticfreejuly.org/

BIOMA biomatravel.org/

HEAL THE OCEAN healtheocean.org

SEA TURTLES CONSERVATION CURACAO seaturtleconservationcuracao.org/

OCEAN CONSERVATION oceanconservation.org

OCEAN CONSERVANCY oceanconservancy.org

SANTA BARBARA CHANNELKEEPER sbck.org

TORTUGAS DE OSA tortugasdeosa.org

GRUPO TORTUGUERO grupotortuguero.org/quienes-somos/

PLASTIC POLLUTION COALITION plasticpollutioncoalition.org/

WORLD TURTLE TRUST & THE HONU PROJECT IN HAWAII world-turtle-trust.org/about.html

BOOKS, DOCUMENTARIES & VIDEOS

Children's Books

One Turtle's Last Straw: The Real-Life Rescue That Sparked a Sea Change by Elisa Boxer (Crown Books for Young Readers, May 10, 2022)

Poppy's Purpose to Prevent Pollution by Melissa Kay Moore (Adventures Publishing, September 15, 2021)

Rocket Says Clean Up! by Nathan Bryon (Random House Books for Young Readers, September 1, 2020)

Saving Tally: An Adventure into the Great Pacific Plastic Patch by Serena Lane Ferrari (Save The Planet Books, October 26, 2019)

Save the Ocean by Bethany Stahl (Save the Earth Book 1, April 15, 2019)

The Green Sea Turtle by Isabel Müller (NorthSouth Books, September 1, 2014)

Thirteen Moons on Turtle's Back: A Native American Year of Moons by Joseph Bruchac and Jonathan London (Puffin Books, August 25, 1997)

We Are Water Protectors by Carole Lindstrom (Roaring Brook Press, March 17, 2020)

Our World Out of Balance: Understanding Climate Change and What We Can Do by Andrea Minoglio (Blue Dot Kids Press, April 13, 2021)

Books for Adults

The Book of Honu: Enjoying and Learning About Hawaii's Sea Turtles by Peter Bennett and Ursula Keuper-Bennett (University of Hawaii Press; August 31, 2008)

Dreaming in Turtle: A Journey Through the Passion, Profit, and Peril of Our Most Coveted Prehistoric Creatures by Peter Laufer, PhD (St. Martin's Press, November 20, 2018)

The Soul of an Octopus: A Surprising Exploration into the Wonder of Consciousness by Sy Montgomery (Atria Books, April 2016)

Thicker Than Water: The Quest for Solutions to the Plastic Crisis by Erica Cirino (Island Press, October 7, 2021)

I Quit Plastics: And You Can Too by Kate Nelson (Lost the Plot, July 1, 2020)

Documentaries & Videos

"My Octopus Teacher," a documentary directed by Pippa Ehrlich and James Reed featuring filmmaker, Craig Foster, about his unusual friendship with an octopus living in a South African kelp forest, who shares the mysteries of her world.

"A Plastic Ocean," a documentary directed by journalist Craig Leeson.

"Bag It," a film by Suzan Beraza.

"On Plastic Straws," a short youtube video by Dr. Christine Figgener, marine conservation biologist.

AUTHOR'S NOTE ~
INSPIRATION & GRATITUDES

Makana is a Gift is inspired by a little boy named Makana, who received his name five months after his birth, common in many traditions—to name a person after their nature or something special is revealed about them.

Makana's sister is the protagonist in *Mermaid Dreams,* one of my other children's books. When he asked if I would write a story about him, I asked if Makana would be a little boy or sea turtle. "Sea turtle," he immediately replied.

I've been carrying a sea turtle story in my heart for years now, having met sea turtles in the waters of Mexico and Costa Rica, and while swimming with the *honu,* the green sea turtles in Hawaii. These magnificent creatures glide gracefully through the water, their peaceful vibration palpable. During one extraordinary encounter, an enormous sea turtle swam straight toward me in a clear shallow bay, where we were suspended momentarily, face to face, eye to eye, in a communion I can only describe as transcendent.

There's no doubt in my mind that these exquisite creatures possess a divine intelligence and inner peace, which ripples throughout the world-wide ocean, resonating with our own inner seas. Their protection from plastics, pollution, and poachers is essential to the preservation of their beneficial presence.

I have deep respect and appreciation for all of the people and organizations devoted to the preservation of sea turtles and all life beneath the sea. (My list of "Resources" is a place to start to learn more about these individual and collective efforts. Follow the current and you will surely find many more!)

From its divine inspiration to publication, a book is blessed by those who support the journey.

I'm grateful to my early readers who offered insights, ideas, and expertise as I developed and refined Makana's story: Jim Maskrey, Kristy Raihn, Meganne Forbes and Sarah Clark; and always to Erika Römer and Colleen McCarthy-Evans, my dream team at Seven Seas Press, for their generous contributions to the overall collaboration. Alexis Cantu's watercolor illustrations have brought Makana's story to life in a way that was beyond my imagination. I'm grateful for the extra depth of her vision. Gracias Marcos Martinez for bringing your voice and spirit to the bilingual translation.

I'm especially grateful to my young friend Makana Ligrano, who inspired the character of the little green sea turtle.

AUTHOR, Janet Lucy, MA, is the award-winning author of *Mermaid Dreams/Sueños de Sirena,* multi-award winning *The Three Sunflowers/Los Tres Girasoles,* and co-author of *Moon Mother, Moon Daughter ~ Myths and Rituals that Celebrate a Girl's Coming of Age.* Janet is the Director of Women's Creative Network in Santa Barbara, California, where she is a teacher and consultant, facilitates women's writing groups and leads international retreats. She can often be found in or near the water. Visit: www.janetlucyink.com.

ILLUSTRATOR, Alexis Cantu is an artist based in The Netherlands, originally from Mexico. She has a degree in Industrial Design from Monterrey Institute of Technology and Higher Education (ITESM). Her passion is art. She is an advocate for women's rights, animals, and environmental protection, especially the ocean. She supports her community by giving free online watercolor workshops. Follow her on Instagram @alexiscantu and visit her at www.alexiscantu.com.

OTHER BOOKS
BY THE AUTHOR AND SEVEN SEAS PRESS

Moon Mother, Moon Daughter ~ Myths and Rituals that Celebrate a Girl's Coming of Age co-authored by Janet Lucy and Terri Allison

Moon Mother, Moon Daughter Moon Circle Facilitator's Guide co-authored by Janet Lucy and Terri Allison (coming in Fall 2022)

The Three Sunflowers by Janet Lucy, illustrated by Colleen McCarthy-Evans

Mermaid Dreams by Janet Lucy, illustrated by Colleen McCarthy-Evans

The Little Blue Dragon written and illustrated by Colleen McCarthy-Evans

Why Am I by Colleen McCarthy-Evans, illustrated by Sarah Dietz

The Crazy Old Maid by Colleen McCarthy-Evans, illustrated by Janneke Ipenburg (coming in Fall 2022)

Versiones bilingües / Bilingual versions:

The Three Sunflowers / Los Tres Girasoles

Sueños de Sirena / Mermaid Dreams

The Little Blue Dragon / La Dragoncita Azul

Por Qué Soy / Why Am I

Makana es un Regalo / Makana is a Gift

About Seven Seas Press:

Seven Seas Press collaborates with authors, artists and translators to create content with sensitivity and depth, that honors and reflects our diverse humanity. Through our nonprofit we create partnerships with local and international organizations, who share our vision to empower, nurture and contribute to the lives of others.

Seven Seas Press is a 501(c)3 Public Charity EIN 83-0792556.

Please visit us at: sevenseaspress.org

SEVEN SEAS
PRESS

Made in the USA
Columbia, SC
02 July 2022

62677576R00031